TREASURE IN AN OATMEAL BOX

Ken Gire

NAVPRESS ®

A MINISTRY OF THE NAVIGATORS

P.O. BOX 6000, COLORADO SPRINGS, COLORADO 80934

The Navigators is an international Christian organization. Jesus Christ gave His followers the Great Commission to go and make disciples (Matthew 28:19). The aim of The Navigators is to help fulfill that commission by multiplying laborers for Christ in every nation.

NavPress is the publishing ministry of The Navigators. NavPress publications are tools to help Christians grow. Although publications alone cannot make disciples or change lives, they can help believers learn biblical discipleship, and apply what they learn to their lives and ministries.

First printing, paperback edition, 1990

Cover art: Michael Garland
Interior illustrations: Patrick J. Welsh

Based on the storyline and characters from the author's earlier book, *The Christmas Duck*, originally published by Mott Media in 1983.

Printed in the United States of America

FOR A FREE CATALOG OF
NAVPRESS BOOKS & BIBLE STUDIES,
CALL TOLL FREE 800-366-7788 (USA)
or 1-416-499-4615 (CANADA)

Contents

*Dedicated to
my mother
and
the memory of my father
in appreciation for teaching me
the important things in life.*

Author

Ken Gire is pursuing a career in writing novels and screenplays in Southern California, where he resides with his wife, Judy, and their children, Gretchen, Kelly, Rachel, and Stephen.

Ken is a graduate of Texas Christian University and Dallas Theological Seminary, and is the author of *Intimate Moments with the Savior* and the *Kid's Praise* adventure series.

The First Day of School

The Hallas family had just moved to North Carolina from Midland, Texas, and already the twins were homesick. To make matters worse, Kim and Kevin arrived in the middle of the school year, and today was their first day of class.

Just the thought of finding her way around a new school, meeting new teachers, and making new friends terrified ten-year-old Kim.

"Hurry, Kevin, it's seven fifteen."

He plunged his spoon into the bowl and shoveled a glob of oatmeal into his mouth. Then another. And another.

"We're gonna miss the bus."

"Be patient, Kim."

"But, Mom, the bus'll be here any minute."

7

Kevin gulped down his orange juice and wiped his mouth with his shirt sleeve.

"We gotta go. *Now*." She plucked her lunch sack from the counter and started to leave.

"Kiss me goodbye."

"Mo-om."

"Quick, you'll be late."

Kim pecked her on the cheek and stomped out the door.

"Save da box, okay, Mom?"

"Hurry, son," she said as she took the round, empty oatmeal box and stored it in the cabinet.

"Wait up!" Kevin tumbled down the porch and ran awkwardly down the driveway.

He had been mentally handicapped since birth. It slowed his mind, slurred his speech, and affected the way he walked. Sometimes none of that bothered Kim. Other times—like today—it did.

She stopped and dug her fists into her hips. When Kevin finally caught up, he blurted out, "Gotta go poddy."

Just then the bus crested the hill.

"You'll have to wait till we get to school."

"I can't."

"You'll *have* to."

They stepped onto the bus, welcomed by the gawking stares of forty strangers. Kim avoided their eyes by searching for an empty seat.

8

"Couple of seats in the back," said the bus-driver.

They walked down the long, narrow aisle, ushered to their seats by the curious whispers of nameless faces. As the bus ground its gears up the hill, Kevin fidgeted in his seat.

"Sit still," Kim whispered.

"Gotta go."

"Shh. You want the whole bus to know?"

Two boys across the aisle stared. Kevin looked at his flustered sister, his eyes wide with worry.

"You'll just have to hold it," Kim said.

Kevin grabbed his pants, and the boys across the aisle leaned forward and stared even harder.

"Not like that," she whispered. "Cross your legs."

When they finally arrived at school, the bus lurched to a stop. All the kids shot out of their seats and clogged the aisle to get out. All, that is, except Kevin.

When Kim looked back, she understood why.

"I twyd to hold it, weally I did."

"Oh, Kevin." Her heart sank. "Here," she said, putting the brown paper sack on his lap, "try to hide it with your lunch sack."

When they entered the classroom, Kevin tried his best to conceal the accident. But as they stood at the teacher's desk to give her their transfer

9

papers, the boy in the front row noticed the large, dark spot on Kevin's jeans.

He whispered to the boy behind him, and the giggling rippled down the rows of wooden desks. Mrs. Hazelwood hushed the class and quickly assigned seats for the two newcomers. As Kevin sat in his, the boy behind him scooted his desk back.

"Pee-ew," he said as he pinched his nose. And that started the whole back row to snickering.

Kim felt like jumping out of her desk and running all the way back to Texas. *Why does he have to be in my class?* she thought to herself. She felt her face turning hot and red. *Why did we have to move to this stupid town anyway?*

At lunch, things got better. A cute boy named Billy smiled at Kim and said "hi." And a few girls invited her to sit at their table. They teased her about her accent, but in a nice kind of way. They asked her to say different words and seemed to enjoy hearing her pronounce them. That made her feel kind of special, like she was a foreign exchange student or something.

Kim looked over at the boys' table and saw Kevin sitting at the far end, eating his sandwich, content in his own little world. She felt bad, seeing him there all by himself. Then she thought, *He's got to learn to make his own friends. I can't always*

10

be there for him. Besides, I need to make friends of my own.

Somehow they survived their first day at the new school. On the bus back, Kim sat next to a girl named Sarah. She had relatives in Odessa, which is just down the highway from Midland. She had visited there last summer, so they had a lot to talk about, and the ride home passed quickly.

Kevin sat alone in the seat across from her, taking in the scenery that passed by the window as he ate leftovers from his lunch sack.

When the bus let them off, they hurried down the driveway, eager to be home.

"How was school today, kids?"

"Good, Mom, weally good."

Mom looked at Kim and read the frustration in her eyes.

"Kevin wet his pants again."

"Oh, yeah," he said, suddenly remembering, "dat part wuddn't so good."

"I was so embarrassed," Kim said as she threw her coat in the chair.

"How did *you* feel about it, Kevin?"

"Wet. Weally, weally wet."

Mom laughed. Kim didn't. "How come Kevin doesn't have a special ed. class like he did in Texas?" she demanded.

"The school here is a lot smaller, sweetheart.

They can't afford classes like that. And besides, they don't have any other kids with the same needs Kevin has."

"So as long as we live in Blake, he'll be in my class, is that it?"

"That's right."

"Even in junior high?"

"Yes."

"How about high school?"

"And high school."

"That's not fair—"

"That's enough, Kim."

"But I don't understand why he can't—"

"*Enough!*"

Kim stared at her. Her mother stared back. She knew the conversation was over, that her mother didn't understand, that she didn't even want to understand. Kim marched off to her room. She threw herself onto the bed. And she cried her complaints into her pillow.

The Accidental Puppy

After Kim had cried out the day's frustrations, Kevin came into the room and sat on his bed. She turned her head away from him.

"I sorry I 'barrassed you."

She muffled her forgiveness into the pillow, "Wasn't your fault."

"I told you I weally had to go."

"I said it wasn't your fault."

"I do better 'morrow, okay?"

She turned her puffy face to see his. It longed for acceptance, for a second chance, for a little sisterly understanding. "Okay." She squeezed out a strained smile, and he beamed like a sunflower.

"I do better 'morrow. You see."

"Maybe if you didn't drink so much orange

juice in the morning, maybe that would help."

"Okay. I can do dat. No pwobwom. I do better 'morrow."

"I know you will, Kevin. I know you will."

Sure enough, he did do better the next day. In fact, the whole day went better. Kim met some more girls. She got a hundred on her spelling test. And several kids came over at recess and asked her all about Texas.

Being the new kid in school wasn't so bad after all.

That afternoon the bus rumbled its way over the gray ribbon of road that threaded through the Blue Ridge Mountains. As it peaked the hill toward home, the bus swerved. There was a thud, and the tires screeched to a stop. It jolted everyone forward, and for a few seconds panic filled the bus.

The driver jerked back the emergency brake and pushed his way through the folding doors. The kids all crowded to the front to see what had happened. They saw him crouched over a black puppy. It looked like a Labrador retriever. The driver turned to the boys squeezing their way through the folding doors.

"Back in the bus. Everyone back in the bus."

After the driver lifted the injured puppy to the side of the road, he hurried all of the kids into their seats. He started the motor, released the brake, and ground the stick shift into gear.

As the bus made its way slowly down the hill, the kids craned their necks to see what damage the bus had done to the puppy. But one by one they turned their gaze away from the road behind them and sat down. Kevin was the only one who continued to press his face against the window. As the dog grew smaller and smaller, his eyes pooled with tears.

The Hallas' mailbox was the next stop. After the bus let the twins out, Kevin ran up the road.

"Where are you going?"

"Da puppy."

"But Kevin—" When he didn't stop, Kim ran to catch him. "Wait for me."

As they got closer, they could see the dog lying on his side, panting. He was still alive. His tongue lolled from his mouth and blood stained his shoulder. He looked up at them with his dark eyes. They were glassy with pain. He whimpered for their help.

"What'll we do?"

"We wap him up in my coat and take him to Dad. He know what to do."

Kevin peeled off his coat and spread it on the ground next to the pup. Gingerly they lifted the dog onto it. They carried him all the way to the front porch, where Kim opened the door and yelled.

"Mom! Mom! Come quick!"

She rushed to the door, drying her hands with a dish towel. Seeing their faces white with fear, her eyes darted to the dog.

"What happened?"

"Da puppy got wun over by da bus. We quick need Dad."

By the time Dad finally got home from work, they had already washed and bandaged the puppy.

"Let's put him in the laundry room for the night," suggested Dad. "It'll be warm in there."

"I'll get him a box," Kim said.

"And I'll get some old towels," Mom added.

Kevin scurried to his room to unplug the night light next to his bed. Then he grabbed the clock on his desk and pulled a book down from his book-shelf. By the time he returned, they had padded an old cardboard box with towels and had already placed the puppy inside.

Kevin plugged the night light into a wall socket. He opened the book to a page with a Labrador retriever pictured and propped it in front of the cardboard box. Then he wound the clock and placed it beside the puppy. He looked up and explained, "So he tink his mommy is next to him."

Dad turned off the light switch, and the soft wash of the night light bathed the room in a golden glow. They looked down at the tired little puppy.

17

As they stared, their hearts melted. In seconds he was asleep. They eased out of the room, whispering their "goodnights" as they all crept off to bed.

Later that night Kevin slipped out from his covers and tiptoed down the hall. The creak of the wood floor followed him. He inched open the laundry room door ever so quietly. After he slipped inside, he knelt beside the cardboard box and folded his hands.

"Pwease, God, pwease help da puppy not to die. Pwease help him to feel betta and git well weal soon. Amen, dear God."

A Mouse
in the House

The next morning the family was awakened by high-pitched whimpering down the hall. Dad, Mom, Kevin, and Kim huddled around the laundry room door where the puppy was trying to scratch his way out.

Dad opened the door. There stood the puppy, wagging his tail and thumping it against the dryer. He stood in one place, shifting his weight to take the pressure off his hurt shoulder. He looked up at them with his dark, eager eyes, almost as if he were waiting for permission to be loved and accepted into the family.

Kevin got on his knees and held out his arms. "Here, boy."

The puppy hobbled over and buried itself in

his embrace. Kevin bent over, showering the dog with kisses. The puppy returned the affection by licking Kevin all over his face.

"Whoa, boy, whoa!" But the dog just kept nuzzling his neck.

"He must be starved," Kim said.

"Why don't you get a bowl of milk for him, Kim," said Mom, "and I'll fry up some leftovers."

The puppy lapped up the milk and shivered with excitement when Mom brought the scraps of food. He wolfed it down fast without hardly even chewing.

"Can we keep him, Dad, huh, can we?"

"I dunno, son."

"Mom?" he asked.

"You promise to clean up after him?"

"Promise," said Kim.

"Cwoss our hearts."

"And bathe him?"

"Chur, we pwomise."

"Then it's all right with me." The twins jumped up and down, clapping their hands. "But before you get too attached to it, we should check with the neighbors. It might belong to someone up the road."

"We gotta give him a name," said Kevin, ignoring Mom's comment.

"How about Midnight?" said Dad.

20

Kevin and Kim looked at each other and wrinkled their noses.

"Blackie?" Again, they rejected his suggestion.

"What about Whimper?" Kim said. But Mom and Dad wrinkled *their* noses at that suggestion.

"Or Wiggles," said Kevin.

"Wiggles. Mmm," said Dad. "What do you say, pooch?"

They looked down at the puppy, who was wagging his tail so hard he almost shook his rear end off.

"I tink he likes it."

So Wiggles it was. Kim made it official by taking a Crayon and printing the name on his box.

Dad talked with some of the neighbors and found that the puppy came from a litter that belonged to Carl and Sadie Matthews. But they were so touched by how Kim and Kevin had cared for the dog, that the elderly couple insisted the kids keep him. Of course, it didn't take much insisting.

Smothered with love, Wiggles recovered quickly. Within two weeks his shoulder healed and his limp went away. But there was one thing that didn't go away—his whimpering.

After everybody went to bed, Wiggles would whine on into the night—sometimes *all* night. Kevin would get up and talk to him through the one-inch space between the floor and the bottom of the door.

Sometimes he would even slip him a little scrap of meat from the fridge. That worked for a while, but the whining seemed to always start up again.

After a few nights of lost sleep, the excitement of a new puppy was beginning to wear a little thin. Dad would get so mad he would yell at the dog from his room. But it usually took him getting up and pounding on the laundry room door to get Wiggles to settle down.

Adjusting to Wiggles required a lot of effort for everyone, especially for Mom. It seemed like every morning she would wake up to some new mess he had created during the night.

One night he opened the dryer, pulled out all the clothes, and chewed up one of her blouses. Another night he tipped over the bleach bottle on her throw rug. Still another night he knocked over the ironing board, which sent him squealing for cover and sent Dad stumbling through the dark hallway with a baseball bat, thinking somebody was breaking into the house.

Of course, that was nothing compared to the night of the mouse.

Every night this mouse would sneak under the laundry room door and nibble away at Wiggles's bowl of dry dog food. And every night Wiggles would sleep through the intrusion. Every night, that is, until *this* night.

22

When the mouse was knee-deep in Purina, munching his way through the dog's food, Wiggles woke up. His black ears pricked up and his eyes locked onto the scratching noise. He lifted a paw over the threshold of his box and crept over to the bowl, sniffing his nose at the rim.

Their eyes met, and they both froze still as statues. But when the mouse twitched his whiskers, they were off to the races. The mouse hurdled the rim and scampered across the slick linoleum floor with Wiggles in hot pursuit. It ran for refuge behind the clothes hamper, but Wiggles nosed it over with a crash that echoed through the house.

Wiggles chased it in a circle and slapped his paw down on its tail. The mouse pawed frantically at the linoleum to get away. Wiggles stuck his nose in the mouse's face and fairly near barked his head off.

But when the pup tried to place his other paw on the mouse, it broke loose and headed for the laundry basket. Squeezing into an opening in the wicker, it stole its way to safety.

Wiggles sniffed and pawed and barked and finally started digging through the mountain of clothes to get to the bottom. When he had scattered half the pile over the floor, the mouse darted into a nearby cabinet.

Wiggles pawed open the cabinet door and sniffed

around for the evasive, little rodent. He knocked over bottle after bottle of detergent, bleach, starch, and a dozen other things.

"Hey, what's going on out there?" hollered Dad from his bedroom at the end of the hall. "Is that you kids?"

"Not us, Dad," Kevin and Kim chorused back.

There was a loud crash, a volley of barks, and they heard Dad throwing off his covers and grumbling, "It's that *dog* again."

When his giant footsteps tramped down the hall, the twins knew there was trouble coming. Dad was hot. Really hot. He kicked open the laundry room door. But before he could say anything, the mouse scurried out down the hall with Wiggles tripping all over himself in chase.

They were both headed toward the master bedroom when Mom turned on the hall light.

"A mouse!" When she screamed, the mouse skidded to a stop just short of her flowing robe. Wiggles tried to stop, but he overshot the mouse and went sprawling into Mom.

Kevin and Kim had bolted out of bed just in time to see the mouse running down the hall toward them with Wiggles barking and sliding all over the wooden floor.

"Ahhhh!" Kim screamed.

"Ahhhh!" screamed Kevin.

They both ran back to their room and jumped onto their beds. The mouse ran under Kevin's. Wiggles scrunched down and crawled after him.

"Where is it?" asked Dad.

Kevin reached down and lifted his bedspread. When he did, the mouse took off running.

"There he goes!" yelled Mom, and she jumped on the bed with Kim. The mouse ran into the wall, raced down the baseboard and into the hall.

"He's getting away," Kim yelled.

"Git him, Dad," hollered Kevin.

Wiggles ran after the mouse. Dad ran after Wiggles. Kevin ran after Dad. Kim ran after Kevin. And Mom was the caboose in this runaway train.

The mouse took a right turn into the darkened living room. Following fast after it, the rest of them collided into each other.

"Hey!" someone shouted. "Watch where you're going!"

"Somebody turn on the light."

"Where's the mouse?" someone else asked.

"The mouse!" yelled Mom. And they all ran out of the dark. First Mom, then Kim, then Kevin. Dad stayed and fumbled along the wall for the light switch.

Wiggles, meanwhile, knocked a lamp off the end table, which sent him whimpering into the hall with the rest of the family.

Dad finally found the light switch. Then the other three timidly poked their heads into the living room.

"Where is it?" Mom asked.

"Halfway to Tennessee by now, I suspect," said Dad.

Suddenly everyone got brave.

"Better be," said Kevin.

"If he knows what's good for him," Kim added.

Wiggles barked in agreement, and they all looked at each other and burst out laughing.

"There it is!" shouted Dad, pointing toward their feet. They all screamed and jumped onto the couch.

A smile crept across his face. "Just kidding."

Mom was the first to hit him. She threw a pillow from the couch, followed by a windmill of fists. The twins were right behind her, pounding and pulling at him, until they finally tackled him and tickled him, rolling all over the living room rug. And Wiggles was right there, too, barking and worming his way into the thick of it.

School Days

Home was to Kevin what the padded cardboard box was to Wiggles — a place that was soft and safe and sheltered from the outside world. School was the outside world for Kevin, and sometimes it could get pretty cold and harsh.

The kids there could be so insensitive — and cruel. But ever since Mrs. Hazelwood had a talk with them the day Kevin was absent, they all started being more considerate.

All except Jerrod Jackson.

Jerrod was the person parents would always use as an example of what you would grow up to be like if you kept on acting the way you did: "Look at Jerrod Jackson. Is that what you want to grow up to be like? Because if you do, then just keep acting the way you're acting now."

Jerrod had been held back two grades, so most of the friends he hung around with after school were in junior high. That put him two grades ahead of a fifth grade vocabulary when it came to bad words.

He was also bigger than the other fifth graders, which he used to his advantage whenever he felt like cutting in line. Or relieving someone of their dessert. Which he did on a regular basis. He was good at that—*real* good.

He was also the only person in the school, besides the janitor, who smoked. Whenever little clouds of smoke billowed in the bathroom stall, you knew it was Jerrod.

One morning Kevin entered the bathroom just as Jerrod exhaled a plume of smoke.

"What're *you* looking at?" he asked as he raked back the sheaf of hair that hung in his face.

"You're smoking," Kevin said with a look of amazement.

"No," Jerrod said sarcastically, "I'm practicing my imitation of a chimney."

As he stubbed out his cigarette and flipped it into the toilet, Kevin turned to leave. He had run up against Jerrod before, and once was enough. But the bully caught up with him and clamped his hand on Kevin's collar bone.

"Where ya think *you're* goin'?"

"Ow. Back to class."

"Weren't thinkin' about snitchin' on me, were ya, big Kev?"

"What?"

"Tellin' the teacher, Dumbo."

"No."

"Good. Last kid that did wished he hadn't."

"I towd you I wuddn't."

Jerrod released his grip and patted Kevin on the shoulder. "Smart boy."

That was Jerrod Jackson — trouble, looking for a place to happen.

All winter Jerrod went out of his way to give Kevin a hard time. At lunch he would go through Kevin's sack, looking for a candy bar or piece of cake. In the hall he would joke about him in front of the other boys. And in class he would shoot spit wads at him when the teacher wasn't looking. But winter finally went away, and along with it went some of Jerrod's hostility.

All winter long the barren branches of oak, maple, and birch trees silhouetted themselves stiffly against the ashen sky. But now spring pierced through the gray. The trees stretched their budding limbs as if just rising from a long nap and yawning themselves awake.

Where the trees thinned out, sunny fields of

31

wildflowers grew. They blanketed the valley like a delicately stitched patchwork quilt. Mingling in the air were the fragrances of a thousand unknown flowers.

Each spring a budding enthusiasm for baseball came over all the boys. This spring was no exception. At recess Mrs. Hazelwood gathered the class on the playground to divide into teams. She then picked two captains and let them choose up sides.

In spite of the fact that nobody liked him, Jerrod was the first one chosen. Because of his size, he could hit the ball farther than anybody in school. And, for thirty minutes a day, that was all that mattered.

One by one the captains grabbed up all the boys except for Kevin. Then they groaned their way through every girl they had to pick. It finally came down to a choice between Kevin and Mary Ellen.

Mary Ellen was frail from a childhood bout with pneumonia and had to carry an inhaler around with her to repell any oncoming attacks of asthma. She couldn't run very far without wheezing, but she could throw the ball pretty well and occasionally could get a hit.

After a mumbled debate, Mary Ellen was chosen. An awkward silence followed.

"Go ahead," the teacher said.

"But the teams are even."

"One more won't make any difference."

"Oh *yeah*," whispered one of the kids.

Kevin looked down and toed the ground with his foot. Kim felt embarrassed—half for him, half for herself. She thought to herself, *It isn't right, him being in my class. If Mom were here, she could see that it isn't right, or fair. Not to the others or to him.*

"Can he keep score? We'll need a scorekeeper," said the captain.

"I'll keep score," said the teacher. "Go ahead, take him."

"Yeah, take him," said the other captain.

"*You* take him."

"It's *your* turn."

"I got one more girl than you," he snapped back.

"Boys, boys," interrupted Mrs. Hazelwood. "Kevin, you be on Tommy's team."

Kevin trudged to the end of the line, shoulders slumped, eyes cast downward. When he took his place, a cloud of defeat settled over the team.

Since there was only one left-hander on the opposing team, Tommy put Kevin in right field. Fortunately, no balls came his way. But he still had to bat. There was no getting around that. He had struck out the first time up. When he came to

33

bat a second time, his team had two outs with the tying run on third.

Kim stood in the outfield as her team started to chatter. "Come on, swing, batter, swing."

The first pitch was high and outside. Kevin swung. And missed. His team groaned behind the backstop.

The pitcher stood confidently on the mound. As he started his wind-up, everyone on the team continued to chatter. Everyone except Kim.

"Come on, batter, swing batter swing, come on now—"

Why are they yelling at him? she thought to herself. *Is winning that important?*

The second pitch hit the dirt in front of the plate. Kevin swung again. Strike two. Kim could hardly bear to watch. The kids behind the backstop shouted their advice.

"Don't swing, Kevin."

"Wait for a good pitch."

"Don't swing. Let him walk you."

As Kevin turned to listen, the pitcher threw the ball. It was low and inside. Ball one.

"Way to go, Kevin!" his teammates shouted.

"Just let the bad ones go by."

"He can't pitch worth beans."

"Four balls and he'll walk ya. Just stand there and don't swing."

Their coaching echoed in his ears as he stood waiting for the next pitch. It was high. Ball two.

His teammates clapped. Even Jerrod got excited. "Way to be, big Kev. Just stand there and let that rag arm walk ya."

The next pitch was outside and in the dirt. His team went wild. The count was now three and two. Three balls and two strikes. One more ball and Kevin would get on first base with a walk. And if he got on base, Jerrod Jackson was next up. All he would have to do is hit a single to bring the runner in from third, and that would tie the game. And if he could knock in Kevin before the bell rang, they would win.

Kevin's team cheered him on from behind the backstop. The other team looked nervous now. A couple of boys from the infield came to talk with the pitcher.

Kim prayed as she trembled in the outfield, *Oh, please, God, let him get a hit, or let him walk, but don't let him strike out.*

The pitcher looked at the runner on third, then squinted at the catcher and nodded. Kevin stood at the plate, waiting for the pitch.

Kevin stood still, determined not to swing. The pitcher released the ball, and it glided right over the plate.

Strike three.

Kevin was out. He stood at the plate, bewildered, as his team took the field. But before he put down his bat, the bell ending recess sounded. The game was over.

Kim ran to him, and he looked to her for some explanation, "But dey towd me not to swing."

When Kevin said that, Jerrod walked by. "We told you not to swing at the bad ones. *The bad ones.* The good ones ya swing at. Doesn't take a lot of brains to figure *that* out."

As Jerrod walked off, all sorts of feelings crowded Kim's mind. She felt angry with Jerrod . . . sad for Kevin . . . guilty for being born normal . . . afraid of what the other kids would say later on . . . embarrassed that her teacher saw somebody in her family flub up . . . frustrated that her mother didn't understand . . . and hurt that God didn't answer her prayer.

Silently she carried all these feelings back to class with her as she slouched in her desk and buried her head in a book she pretended to be reading.

Rainy Day Sunshine

Saturday morning Kevin and Kim woke to the sound of rain tapping on their window. It was a gray, lazy day with nothing special to get up for, so Kim turned away from the window, lost herself in the tangle of covers, and buried her head in her feather pillow.

But soon the smells of bacon and eggs and toast came wandering into the room, tempting her to the kitchen. When the coffee started to perk, it overpowered the other smells. Although she hated the taste, the smell of coffee was one of her favorite smells.

It meant that Mom and Dad were awake, getting the house warmed up. It meant that you could roll over and go back to sleep, because they were

39

there looking after things. The smell of coffee. Mmmm, how she loved it. Especially on lazy, rainy mornings.

The morning bliss was short-lived, though, shattered by a wide-awake, ready-for-play dog. He jumped onto Kevin's bed and licked his face. Kevin threw his covers over him, but that didn't stop Wiggles. He grabbed a mouthful of Kevin's blanket and started pulling.

Kim jerked around in her bed, irritated they had interrupted her peaceful morning's sleep. "Knock it off. It's Saturday!"

"Come on, Wiggles, top it. Top it *wight* now." Kevin spoke firmly, like Dad did whenever the dog got a little too frisky. But Wiggles wasn't fooled for a minute. Finally Kevin pushed him off the bed. Wiggles then burrowed under the bedspread and snuffled his cold nose against Kevin's bare feet.

"Otay, otay, I getting up. Otay, top it. I getting up."

Wiggles paid special attention to Kevin. Why, Kim didn't know. She only knew that it seemed as if he were Kevin's dog rather than belonging to both of them. That didn't seem right. After all, they both shared the chores in taking care of him. It seemed only fair that they should share his affection, too.

In fact, she did more than her share of the

chores. She was always taking up the slack for Kevin whenever he forgot to do something. And he forgot a lot.

She fed the dog in the morning. Kevin fed him after school—which is a lot easier, because you're not sleepy after school like you are in the morning. And you're not rushed either. They both washed him, but Kim did most of the work. Kevin played in the water too much to be of any real help. Kim had to clean the laundry room once a week, while Kevin had to brush Wiggles' coat. She would have traded jobs in a minute. Hers was more work and a lot less fun.

These thoughts followed her to the table and somehow kept breakfast from tasting as good as it smelled from the bedroom.

"Going to the feedstore. You kids want to come?"

"No thanks," Kim said.

"Chur, I go wit you, Dad."

Kevin scraped his plate and stuffed the last bit of jellied toast into his mouth. He plopped onto the floor and dangled a piece of bacon in front of Wiggles. His wet, eager nose sniffed the air, then nipped the tasty morsel right out of Kevin's hand.

"Whaddya say, boy? Wanna go?"

"He wants to stay here," said Kim.

"He want ta go. See, he all 'cited 'bout going."

41

"He's not excited about going; he's excited about the bacon you're giving him."

"Let's not make a big deal about it, Kim," said Mom.

She turned and snapped, "Well it *is* a big deal."

"Why don't you go with us?" said Dad.

"I don't wanna go. I just wish for once . . . . Never mind." She scraped back her chair and left for her room.

She plopped on the bed and bunched up her pillow. She lay there, pouting as she watched the rain weep against the window. The room was a mess. Mostly Kevin's stuff. Clothes on the floor. Books scattered about.

The rain started to let up when Mom came into the room. She sat on the side of the bed and softly moved her hand over Kim's back. She didn't say anything for a long time, just looked out the window.

"Something peaceful about the rain, isn't there?"

Kim didn't answer. She just dug her chin into the pillow and waited for the lecture. But the lecture never came.

"Want me to go?" she asked.

"If you want."

"Do you want me to?"

"It's a free country."

She touched a strand of hair hanging in Kim's face and swept it gently in place.

"I know it's hard, sweetheart."

Kim turned to face her. "*Do* you? Do you know what it's like to have kids talk behind your back because you have a retarded brother? And think maybe that you might be a little retarded, too. That it runs in the family. Do you know what it's like to have him strike out every time he gets up to bat? Do you know what it's like to always have to pick up after him? Just look. Those aren't *my* clothes on the floor. Or my books all over everywhere. Or my toys.

"I have to clean up after him, too."

"But you don't have to go to school with him."

"No. You're right. I don't."

Once Kim started talking, she couldn't stop. Everything that had been bottled up inside her just spewed out.

"You don't know how I feel, Mother. You don't know what it's like having Kevin and Wiggles playing together all the time and leaving me the odd man out."

"Who else has Kevin got to play with besides you and Wiggles? Who invites him over to play? Who asks him to spend the night? Nobody. People invite you all the time."

"It's not my fault I was born normal."

43

"And it's not his fault he wasn't, so don't blame him."

"I don't blame him. I don't blame anybody. I just wish you and Dad could understand."

"Understand what?"

"What it's like to be the sister of a retarded brother."

Mom turned to stare out the window, and a long pause lingered between them. She took a deep breath and, with halting words, turned to her daughter.

"Do you know what it's like . . . what it's like to be the *mother* of a retarded son? To know that he will never play sports as good as the other boys. That he won't be included in their games. Or their conversations. Or their friendships. That he won't date, won't—" She sighed. "Won't go to the senior prom. To know that no matter how many times he falls in love, he'll only come away with a broken heart. That he'll probably never marry or—"

Her voice cracked. She looked away to the window, to the sun filtering in through the lace curtains. A tear spilled from her eye and made a wet line down her cheek. "Or have kids of his own—"

Her lower lip started to quiver. A terrible feeling came over Kim as she watched her mother crumble before her eyes. She tried to understand the pain her mother carried so deep inside. She tried desperately.

Mom stumbled over her words as she continued, "Kids he will never be able to play with, or watch grow up . . . kids he'll never be able to talk with—"

She buried her face in her hands and broke down completely. Kim sat up and tried to think of the right thing to say. But no words came. She just held her mother and cried with her.

Growing Up

From that time on, Kevin and Kim spent more time together. Every weekend they played outside. Catching monarch butterflies. Collecting leaves for their scrapbooks. Pressing wildflowers between pages in books. Exploring all the nooks and crannies the valley had to offer.

Wiggles tagged along, of course. He helped chase down butterflies and sniffed out a few rabbits and squirrels along the way.

This weekend, though, Dad had something else to keep the twins occupied—the barn.

It was a red barn, old and weathered. Some of the planks had warped at the ends and had worked out the nails that held them in place. After a few weekends of Dad nailing, scraping, and sanding, he introduced them to what he called "the pleasures of paint."

Those pleasures lasted for maybe an hour. After that, the novelty of it all wore off pretty quick. Paint dripped down the handle of the brushes and onto their hands. Then it started to dry and get sticky. And the higher the sun rose, the hotter it got. Sweat beaded their foreheads and trickled to sting their eyes. By lunchtime, they were ready to trade in their brushes for a can of turpentine and a hot bath.

While the family ate lunch, Wiggles took to chasing chickens. Great sport, chickens. And a lot less humiliating than chasing mice. Wiggles loved the feathers flying in the air and the confusion of the hens running into each other. To his credit, he never hurt any. His fun was putting a scare into them, seeing them flap their wings, and hearing them squawk.

Mom heard the commotion from the kitchen and failed to see the fun in it all. She threw open the screen door.

"Quit chasing those chickens, dog. Stop him, Pete. Don't let him carry on like that."

"He's not hurting any of 'em, Lucy—just having a little fun."

"If they get excited, they'll stop laying."

"Wiggles!" he yelled his commands. "Come

here! Leave those chickens alone!"

The blur of black hair stopped in its tracks. A flurry of feathers floated down around the dog. He barked a couple more times just to give the hens a final scare.

"Git over here!"

Wiggles tucked his tail and slinked over to Dad, eyes downcast and fearful. Kim tore off some of her sandwich to let him know the whole family wasn't mad. He gobbled it down, and that seemed to do the trick. He perked right up.

He sniffed the air. Kim thought it was for more of her sandwich. But he jerked his head around and, with ears alert, stood motionless.

They all looked up in time to see a skunk turning the far corner of the barn. He waddled under the ladder and sniffed the freshly painted barn suspiciously.

"That ain't no chicken," said Dad under his breath. And that's all the encouragement Wiggles needed. He sprinted after it.

The skunk hurried through the barn door with Wiggles running in after him, barking loud enough to hatch a whole henhouse full of eggs. But no sooner had he run into the barn than he ran right out again, yelping so pitifully that it sounded like someone had thrown a skillet full of hot grease on him.

49

He whined as he rubbed his nose onto the grass. And after he rolled over and over to wipe the smell from his coat, he ran over to the porch.

"Run for it!" yelled Dad. And they scattered in four different directions.

Wiggles ran back and forth between them as if he were chasing chickens. He caught up with Kim first and barked for help. He stunk to high heavens—enough to make your eyes water. Kim pinched her nose and shooed him away.

"Go away. Go to Kevin."

Kevin saw him coming and ran awkwardly toward the ladder. He started climbing the rungs, but Wiggles was on his heels, climbing right behind him.

"Oh, you tink! You tink bad. Go 'way, git." Kevin pushed his foot at the dog and climbed farther up.

While the two of them were raising a ruckus, the skunk ambled out of the barn. Wiggles saw him and ran off in the opposite direction as the skunk disappeared around the corner.

Kevin and Kim ran to the front porch as fast as they could and squeezed through the front door, slamming it safely behind them as they did.

"Whew," Kim sighed.

"I never smelt tink like dat. *Never*."

When they looked up, Mom was holding an

extra-large can of tomato juice and two towels.

"What dat for?"

"To clean the smell off the dog."

"Tomato juice?" Kim asked.

"Best thing to get rid of skunk odor," she said. "Here." She thrust the towels and juice at them.

"You wouldn't send us out there, would you?"

"I would, and I am."

"But, Mom, he tink so bad," objected Kevin.

"You promised to keep him clean, remember?"

That night as Kim and Kevin lay in their beds, they relived the day's adventure. They talked and laughed, and Kim felt a deep tenderness for her brother as she listened to his bent words that tried to come out straight.

Kevin reached out across the chasm that separated their beds and extended his arm so she could softly tickle it. It was a ritual they went through every night, taking turns stroking each other's arms with the silken tips of their fingers.

When Kim finished, she extended her arm to him.

"My turn."

There was no answer.

"It's my turn, Kevin. Kevin?"

But he was already asleep.

* * *

After church the next morning, they went to Carl and Sadie Matthews' for lunch. The Matthews lived down the road in a white, clapboard house with forest-green shutters and a red-brick walkway lined with daffodils.

They never had kids of their own. They adopted one once. A baby boy. But he died early on. They never adopted again. The twins saw the boy's headstone out back under the oak tree. He died a long time ago, when the Matthews were in their prime. Now they were old. Gray. Wrinkled. Bent over a bit. But they were still in love, and they hadn't forgotten how to laugh.

They laughed a lot around the table that Sunday afternoon. They laughed about the pleasures of paint, about slow-walking skunks and stinky black dogs and the wonders of tomato juice.

During a lull in the laughter, Mr. Matthews moved his chair away from the table and looked over his glasses.

"Got a little something for you, Kevin."

Kevin beamed and started to shake with excitement.

Mr. Matthews got up from the table. It was with some effort for his bones were old and tired. He opened a compartment in his roll-top desk and brought back something wrapped in his hand.

He opened his palm to reveal a dog he had carved from wood. It was two inches long and painted black to look like Wiggles.

"Oh, tank you, Mizter Matt! Tank you so much!" Kevin threw his arms around the man's frail waist. "I wuv it. It's da best pwesent I could ever want, ever and ever."

Mr. Matthews didn't have anything for Kim. It was an oversight. He probably just got so excited about bringing a smile to Kevin's face that he forgot about Kevin's normal, twin sister.

But that was okay. It didn't matter. For Kim, seeing Kevin so happy was present enough.

Kim looked over at Mom.

She smiled tenderly.

Kim smiled back. And she understood.

Fourth of July
Picnic

School ended in June and threw open the doors to summer. Summertime was a great relief, like when you come home from church and take off your Sunday clothes. That kind of relief.

For a kid, it meant you could go barefoot and run around in cutoffs and T-shirts. It meant nobody cared if your hair wasn't in place or if you went to bed without a bath.

It meant waking up to woodpeckers, chasing fireflies at dusk, and listening the night away on a porch swing to the calls of varmints and the gossip of far-away frogs. It meant wading in creeks and skipping flat rocks and fishing lonesome ponds.

The highlight of summer in the valley was the Fourth of July picnic. Everybody in the valley attended. Maybe it was the food that brought them. Fried chicken. Potato salad. Fresh vegetables from backyard gardens. Homemade rolls. Corn on the cob. Peach cobbler. Deep-dish apple pie.

Or maybe it was the music. Small bluegrass bands with fiddles and banjos that set the most arthritic knee stomping to the rhythm.

Or maybe it was the competition—the dessert "bake-off" for the women and the pie-eating contest for the men.

Or maybe it was the games. Sack races. Egg toss. Horse shoes. Wheelbarrow races. Greased pig chase.

Or maybe it was just being able to see everybody after a month off from school.

Whatever the attraction, the picnic was a huge success. Handmade quilts blanketed the ground. End-to-end card tables formed one long buffet. And the activities were in full swing.

"Hey, Carl, Sadie," called Dad as the Matthews finished unloading their car. "Come join us. We got a nice, shady spot over here."

Kevin ran to help with their picnic basket.

"That's okay, Kevin. I can get it."

"It's no pwobwom, Mizter Matt. I hep you." And he took one of the handles to lighten the load.

Wiggles came along and sat on the corner of

56

the quilt, waiting for a few tasty morsels to come his way.

"I git you someting, boy. Come on."

Wiggles jumped to his feet and followed Kevin to the table. Kim followed after them.

As bad luck would have it, Jerrod Jackson was there piling up his plate with seconds.

"Hewwo, Jehwed," said Kevin. Kim said nothing, pretending to be looking away at the sack races.

"Well, if it isn't my old buddy, Kevin," he said sarcastically. "How's life in the slow lane?"

Kim wheeled around, teeth gritted, eyes glaring. "Shut up, Jerrod, just shut your big, fat mouth!"

Jerrod put his plate down and came toward her with a scowl on his face. "And who's gonna make me?"

Kevin pushed his arm out to stop his advance. "Don't, Jehwed, pwease. Pwease don't."

Jerrod stopped. He looked at Kevin, pushed his hand away, and turned to pick up his plate.

Kevin got a plate of his own and navigated the islands of food while trying to steer clear of Jerrod. Kim avoided him by going around the other side.

As they worked their way down the table, Wiggles' patience exhausted itself, and he begged for a hand-out. Kevin threw him a roll, but as he did, he stumbled into Jerrod. The flimsy plate crumpled against the boy's back, and the food smeared against his shirt. Jerrod jerked around.

"Why don't you watch where you're goin', *retard!*" he snapped.

Kim's anger exploded, and she upended the card table. Jerrod fell to the ground, buried under an avalanche of food. She stood with her hands fisted against her hips and her eyes glowering down at him.

"Don't ever say that again. Ever."

Jerrod threw some of his newly acquired curse words at her and started to get up. But Wiggles was right there in his face, baring his teeth and growling. A sudden terror flashed across the boy's face, and he froze. Seeing the overturned table, Dad came running.

"What happened?"

There was a strained silence. Dad looked at Kim, then at Jerrod, then at Kevin.

"Accident, Dad, dat's all."

"An accident?"

"We cwean it up, don't worwy."

Dad turned to Jerrod. "You okay, son?"

Without looking up, he wiped some food from his face and mumbled, "I'm okay."

Dad helped them clean things up. He didn't say a word. Nor did the twins. He knew it wasn't

58

an accident. And they knew he knew it wasn't an accident. But he didn't say anything. Not then. Not ever.

But just before he left, he looked at Kim and asked, "You okay, hun?"

She nodded.

And he smiled and patted her on the shoulder.

Kevin's Special Place

When the Hallases got home, it was late afternoon. After they unloaded the car, Kim went to clean up and Kevin went for a walk with Wiggles.

They stopped at a special place of theirs under a huge oak tree that stood about fifty yards from the barn. It was a quiet place, a place Kevin went to often. He went there to rest, to think, to dream, to talk out his frustrations, sometimes to cry, but most of all, he went there just to be alone.

"Otay, boy. Wet's west awhile." Wiggles wagged his tail in approval.

Kevin dug into his pocket and pulled out the woodcarving Mr. Matthews had made for him. He set it on the ground and reached over to pet the dog.

"Da sky is pwetty today, huh? Wook up der."

He pointed to a billow of clouds. "Dat cwoud in da sky. It wook wike a face." Hc kept looking and straining to see whose face. "Jehwed. It wook wike Jehwed Jackson."

Wiggles growled.

A long silence followed as Kevin folded his hands behind his head and watched the wind slowly soften the shape of the cloud.

"Wook, boy. Da cwoud. It not wook wike Jehwed anymow. It nicer now. Tink dat could happen to Jehwed someday, him git nicer?"

Kevin looked a long time into the sky. Wiggles sat next to him, content to just be by his side. In the peaceful silence Kevin heard something that captured his attention.

He got up and looked around. It sounded like it was coming from the bush a little ways behind him. He put his finger on his lips to shush Wiggles and then tiptoed over to the bush.

He parted the leafy branches and discovered a bird nest, where four babies stretched their necks and chirped their lungs out. They were all flesh and no feathers. Their skin was pink and transparent. Their eyes were closed and looked all bug-eyed. Their blood vessels were a delicate weave of red and blue across the surface of their skin.

Wiggles sniffed the nest. Kevin tapped him on the snout. "Top it."

Seeing them struggle, so new to the world and helpless, Kevin's heart went out to them. He bent over for a closer look and saw that one of the babies had something wrong with its right wing and leg. And its neck didn't seem strong enough to support its head. It kept falling over to the side.

Kevin reached to pick up the bird. He didn't know what to do with it; he just felt it needed to be held. As he reached into the nest, the other birds chirped more frantically. They all opened their beaks, expecting food.

Kevin placed the deformed bird in the palm of his hand. It lay on its side, breathing hard, and Kevin could feel the warm throb of its life in his hand.

"You be otay when your mommy git back. Don't worwy." He petted the bird lightly. Then he bent down to show it to Wiggles, instructing him, "Don't wick it or anyting. Just wook."

He sniffed all around Kevin's palm but was careful not to touch the bird.

"I hold you till your mommy git back, if you want me to." The bird started to chirp again and shivered in his hand. "Otay. I put you back wit your bwudders and sisters den. Dey will take care of you till your mommy come home."

Kevin gently placed the little deformed bird back in its nest, and the others stretched their necks again and cried out.

"You birdies gonna get bad soar thwoats if you keep yelling your heads off wike dat."

When Kim approached, he had just put the bird back in its nest. "Time to come in, Kevin. Mom wants us to take baths tonight."

Kevin motioned her over to see his discovery. "Wook what we found, Kim. Birdies. Four of dem."

"Wow. They're just babies."

"Thwee are all otay, but one is bent." He pointed to the deformed bird.

"He'll probably die."

"Die?" Kevin asked.

"The parents usually push any defective ones out of the nest . . . or just stop feeding it so they'll have more food for the babies that are healthy."

"Why?" Kevin's voice was troubled and shaken.

"Survival of the fittest, the law of the jungle."

"Dat not a good law," said Kevin sternly.

"It's not good or bad, really. It's just how things are."

"Would Mom and Dad do dat to me?"

"What ever gave you that idea?"

"Well, dat birdie, he's wike me, isn't he?"

Kim looked away and tried to ignore the question, but Kevin wouldn't let her.

"Isn't he?"

"A little," she answered.

"Dey wouldn't do dat to me, would dey?"

"No, Kevin. They would never do that to you."

She smiled, and he breathed a sigh of relief.

"Race you home."

Kevin's face suddenly brightened. "You give me a head tart?"

"How much of a head start?"

"Count to ten," he said.

"Okay. On your mark. Get set. Go!" Kevin took off running, along with Wiggles, while Kim stood counting.

"One . . . two . . . three . . . four . . ."

He'll never win a track meet with form like that, she thought to herself as she watched his hobbled gait.

"five . . . six . . . seven . . ."

He would probably never win much of anything in life.

"eight . . . nine . . ."

Except hearts.

"Ten."

And he would win a lot of those.

"Ready or not, here I come!"

The Wandering

The next morning a chill settled in on the valley, bringing with it a dense fog. The whole family commented about it from the breakfast table as they drank hot chocolate and ate oatmeal.

Over the mounds of oatmeal they sprinkled brown sugar and topped it off with a pat of real butter. The butter melted down the sides like streams of yellow lava. And upon all of this they poured a little fresh cream. The smells mingled together in wisps of steam that ascended from the bowls. They filled the room with a delicious aroma and chased away the outside chill.

The cylindrical oatmeal box stood plumply on the kitchen counter, somewhat out of place next to the other squarely boxed cereals. Kevin looked

67

over at it when he finished and asked, "Is da box empty?"

"Almost," said Mom.

"Tave it for me when it is, otay?"

"I'll put it with the rest."

"Tanks."

When breakfast was over, they all went their separate ways. Mom did dishes. Dad puttered around in the garage. Kim went to her room to read. Kevin decided to get a pile of picture books to pass the time on this foggy day.

By mid-afternoon he completed his pile. It was time to look for something else to do. He reached into his pocket, looking for his wooden dog.

It wasn't there.

He checked the other pocket. It wasn't there either. Suddenly he remembered where he left it—under the oak tree yesterday, where he was gazing at the clouds.

He knew Mom wouldn't let him go out in the fog, so instead of asking her and getting a no, he quietly inched open the back door and slipped out.

The fog was everywhere. The usual outside noises seemed to hush in its presence, almost out of reverence—or fear. Kevin heard a few muffled sounds from afar off, but otherwise it was silent and still. The cows were quiet. The horses were quiet. The birds were quiet. Or if they were making any noise, the fog absorbed it all like some huge ball of cotton.

The fog was so thick that Kevin could only see a few feet in front of him. But in places the fog would thin out, and he could see farther.

He started toward the direction of the tall oak tree, which was about fifty yards from the barn. He couldn't see the tree so he just started from the corner of the barn and charted his way the best he could.

Every few yards he had to stop and get his bearings. But after about twenty yards or so, he couldn't tell which way was forward and which was back. That's when he started getting scared.

He wanted to call for Dad, but he knew he would just get into trouble for going out without asking. He plodded forward instead. His steps were unsteady. A few times he stumbled. Droplets from the fog condensed around his neck and forehead. His face felt cool and clammy.

He took tentative steps, testing the ground in front of him as he walked. Then he saw it. The craggy branches of the half-dead oak, reaching out into the fog like bony fingers.

Kevin breathed a sigh of relief. He took bolder steps now, and within a minute he was there. He made it.

Immediately he went about searching for the

little black woodcarving. He touched the trunk of the tree and tried to remember where he had sat yesterday in relation to it. He got on hands and knees and began combing his fingers through the grass.

But he couldn't find it. What he found instead was the paw print of an animal. Then another. And another. He didn't know what kind of animal it was, only that it had claws.

From behind him he heard the bushes rustle. His body stiffened. His heart raced.

He heard a frightened cry. He turned and stood up. His eyes strained to pierce the white curtain of fog. He heard it again. This time it sounded more like a snuffling whimper. For a second the curtain parted, and he saw it.

A baby bear.

The bear turned and looked at him. It was lost, scared, helpless. And it was the cutest little baby bear Kevin had ever seen.

"You wook afwaid as me, wittle bear. Wooks wike you got wost in da fog, too."

Kevin crept toward it with deliberate steps so as not to alarm it. Slowly he extended his hand. The bear sniffed it. Sensing that the bear realized he meant no harm, Kevin petted it. That seemed to calm it down.

"Come, I take you back to your mommy."

Kevin reached down and cradled the bear in his arms. The bear resisted. "Don't be afwaid. I won't huwt you."

Maybe it was the soft tone of his voice. Maybe it was the tender way he cuddled it in his arms. Or maybe it was something animals can just sense about a gentle-spirited person. Whatever it was, the bear relaxed and let Kevin hold it.

"You heavier dan you wook, baby bear, know dat? A wot heavier."

Kevin started up the gentle slope of the foot-hills to look for the cub's home. After about five minutes of hiking uphill, Kevin was exhausted.

"Whaddya say we west awhile? I'm pooped out."

He put the cub down on a large, flat rock. It sniffed the air as if it smelled something familiar.

"You wemember dis pwace?"

The cub raised its muzzle and called out into the fog.

"Pwetty good for a wittle guy like—"

"Rooooaaaarrrr!" An adult bear returned the cub's call. Its roar knifed through the fog as it came uphill from the direction of the old oak tree. The sharp edge of the roar ran down Kevin's spine and sent chills running all over him.

A scene from *Goldilocks and The Three Bears* flashed across his mind—the one where the family of bears discovered Goldilocks sleeping in the baby bear's bed. And how, once discovered, she jumped out of the bed and ran away.

Suddenly, the instinct to run shot through Kevin.

"Gotta go, wittle fewwa. You be otay; your mommy is—"

Another roar blasted through the fog, this time stronger—which meant the bear was closer.

Kevin left the cub and ran clumsily up the forested slope. Loose rocks under his feet hampered his ascent, and thin limbs whipped across his face.

He panted heavily, gasping for breath. He came to a pile of boulders that looked as if it might provide a fortress from the advancing bear.

Kevin climbed awkwardly over the boulders and lost his footing. One foot slid between two rocks. An arrow of pain shot from his ankle to his hip.

Grimacing, he pulled at his foot to dislodge it. It wouldn't budge. He tried pushing the rocks away. But they were buried deep in the ground, and they wouldn't budge either. He rested his weight against the boulder and paused to catch his breath.

"Arrgrgrgrrr!"

The bear was not content just to find its cub. It was now looking for the one who had taken it.

"ARRGRGRGRGRRRR!" The roar was louder, angrier. The bear was closing in.

72

Kevin pulled his leg with both arms and with all the strength he had left in his thigh. The foot loosened but only after the rock had gashed his ankle, exposing the bone. He finally pulled it free and limped as fast as he could to the dead oak that stood between the boulders.

He stepped on a low branch, but it was so brittle, it broke. He made another attempt. He climbed as high as he could, breaking a few of the smaller branches along the way.

Without thinking, he put his weight on the injured ankle. It buckled beneath him, painfully, and he started to fall. But on his way down, he grabbed onto a limb and pulled himself up.

He wrapped his arms around the branch and hung on for dear life. He held on so hard that the rough bark scraped his cheek.

His heart pounded. He tried desperately to catch his breath. Then he saw it. And his heart almost stopped.

The bear lumbered to the base of the boulders, sniffed around, then stood upright. It must have been seven feet tall. It looked all around, but it didn't see Kevin.

Kevin's heart beat so fiercely he was sure the bear could hear it. The bear looked at the base of the tree. Kevin held his breath. It seemed like forever. He felt his lungs would burst.

The bear crawled over the boulders and sniffed the place where Kevin's foot had been trapped. It raised its head and let out a deafening roar.

Kevin exhaled, took another deep breath and held it.

The bear angled his head upward and caught sight of Kevin. Their eyes met. Neither moved a muscle. It seemed like an eternity to Kevin.

The bear was the first to move. It let out a volcanic roar and lunged toward the base of the tree.

"Oh, God, hep me, pwease hep me! Pwease, God, oh, God, pwease!"

The bear wrapped its burly arms around the trunk and started its climb. Kevin struggled to reach the next branch. It was no use. Too high. And his ankle was too weak for him to jump.

Kevin looked in fear as the bear climbed closer. Its head was massive. Its teeth, ferocious. Its eyes, wild and angry. With its huge right paw, the bear took a swipe at Kevin's foot.

Kevin screamed at the top of his lungs, "GO AWAAAAAAY!"

The scream was so loud and intense that it startled the weighty bear. It shifted its weight, and when it did, the dead branch it was standing on snapped.

As the bear fell, its legs caught the lowest branch and flipped it around so that its head came crashing down against the boulder below.

Kevin stared in disbelief. He hugged the tree and, with his face pushed hard against its bark, started to cry. Tears ran down his scratched and dirty face.

After they had dried and he had caught his breath, Kevin peered down at the bear. A stream of blood trickled from its head.

He felt safe to begin his descent. But as he made his way down the tree, out of the corner of his eye he saw the huge pile of fur move. He stood on the branch, motionless. His eyes widened. His heart started pounding again.

He stared long and hard.

The chest moved. The bear was breathing.

The Search

Dusk was deepening in the valley, and Kevin realized he would have to wait in the tree until someone came looking for him. He shinnied back up to a branch where he could wait safely until help came.

He leaned back against the branch to rest for a few minutes. He was exhausted. His nerves had been so frazzled that it drained every bit of energy. He moved around on the branch and got comfortable. Before long, he was asleep.

By now, night had fallen. Back at the farmhouse the lights from the windows diffused into the fog. Inside, Lucy was fixing dinner.

"Honey, will you get the kids? Dinner's almost ready."

Dad poked his head into the twins' room, where Kim was sprawled across her bed, reading a book.

"Time to eat."

"Be there in a sec. One more page and I'll be finished with the chapter."

Dad looked around the room. "Where's Kevin?"

"Not in here. Maybe he's in the living room."

"Kevin! Time to eat!" he called down the hall.

No answer.

"Check the barn," Mom said, worry starting to well up inside her.

Dad unlatched the barn door. No lights were on. "You in here, Kevin?" All he heard was the hollow sound of his own voice.

By now, Dad started getting worried. He trotted back to the house, where Mom stood framed in the doorway.

"He's not there."

Mom cupped her hands and called out into the night, "Kevin! KEVIN!"

Dad called out, too, "KEVIN! KEEEVVVIIIN!"

Still no answer.

Dad got his high-beam flashlight and went out into the night with Wiggles keeping step beside him. The first place he looked was Kevin's special place at the old oak tree. Once there, Wiggles started barking.

"What is it, boy? Was he here?"

Wiggles sniffed the ground and found the woodcarving. Dad picked it up, then searched the area with his light. He found a set of Kevin's footprints. Then he found the bear tracks. Both sets.

"KEVIN! KEVIN!"

He listened for an answer, but when none came, he sprinted home. Instead of following him, Wiggles dashed up the hill, hot on Kevin's scent.

Dad arrived at the kitchen door out of breath. He went straight to the gun cabinet and got his Winchester.

"What is it, Pete?" Kim looked over at Mom and could see she was scared.

"He's outside somewhere, and there's a bear out there with him."

"I'm going with you."

"Too dangerous," he said as he pocketed a handful of bullets.

"I'm going," she demanded.

"No."

Dad ran out, and the screen door slapped shut behind him. The beam from his flashlight bobbed over the pasture as he ran, illuminating the fog. When he got to the oak tree, he shined his light on the tracks and followed them uphill.

"Wiggles! WIIIIGGGGLLLEESS!"

In the distance he heard two barks, as if a

reply. Dad yelled out again, but this time there was no answer.

Wiggles was too hot on the scent to wait for Dad to catch up. He forged ahead, sniffing his way up the heavily wooded slope.

At last, he came to the area where Kevin was. The strong scent of bear overpowered the human scent. Wiggles surveyed the boulders with caution. He knew Kevin was close but not how close. He barked once, twice, then again.

Kevin awoke with a start and almost fell out of the tree.

"Up here, boy! I up here!"

The dog ran to the base of the tree and jumped up and down, barking his head off.

"Quiet, boy. Der's a bear lying on da wock. Top barking."

As Kevin worked his way down the tree, he stopped to look at the boulder below.

There was no bear.

All that was there was a dark stream of blood.

He eased down the trunk of the tree and threw his arms around his dog.

"Tank you for finding me, boy. Tank you, oh, tank you."

Wiggles lapped his face with his tongue and wagged his tail wildly. But a rustling noise from the bushes abruptly interrupted the reunion.

Kevin hobbled behind the tree to hide. "Come on, boy," he whispered, but the dog wouldn't come.

Wiggles turned and growled just as the bear stood up and parted the bushes. Its head was matted with blood, and it staggered as its eyes locked on the dog.

Wiggles bared his teeth, a white row of drawn daggers that stood out sharply against his black coat. He growled menacingly. The bear growled back, and it was clear the odds were against the dog, in spite of the bear's head wound.

With unsteady footing, the bear weaved its way to attack the dog. But the black lab struck first. He took a running start and lunged at the bear, knocking it off its feet. It struggled to get up, and as it did, the dog's teeth plunged into its neck. Wiggles hung on like a steel trap and shook his head violently.

The bear righted itself and clubbed the dog with one crushing, downward blow. Wiggles fell to the ground and didn't get up.

"Wiggles," gasped Kevin.

When he said this, the bear caught sight of him hiding behind the trunk. Kevin couldn't climb the tree. He couldn't run. He looked around frantically. On the ground near him he spotted a large rock.

As the bear slowly came his way, Kevin picked

up the rock with both hands. He held it over his head, cocked and ready to throw. If the bear didn't stand up, he had a chance at hitting it on its head wound. And maybe, just maybe, the rock would crack the skull.

Kevin's arms quivered from the strain of holding the rock so high and for so long. The rock weaved back and forth. Kevin tried to steady it, but when he did, he slipped and fell. Pain from his ankle shot through the whole one side of his body like a jagged jolt of electricity.

The bear kept coming—slowly and unsteadily—but it kept on coming. With great effort and pain, Kevin stood up. He hoisted the rock over his head.

The bear was twenty feet away. Now fifteen. Kevin cocked his arms. Twelve feet away. Now ten. Kevin took careful aim.

But suddenly the bear stood on its hind legs, towering over Kevin and his rock. He trembled as the bear let out a terrifying roar.

"ARRRRGRGRGRGRGRG—"

A shot cracked through the night and silenced the roar. The bear staggered back. Blood spilled from a hole in its chest. It regained its footing and roared even more ferociously.

"ARRRRRGRGGRGRGRGRGRGRG—"

Another shot rang out. Another hole in its

chest. But it still kept coming . . . nine feet . . . eight . . . seven.

Another shot, this one hitting it in the neck. The bear fell on all fours. But it regained its balance and kept coming. Six feet . . . five feet . . . four. . . .

The Homecoming

Kevin saw the blood pouring from the bear's head. He hurled the rock. It hit the wound squarely, and the bear dropped in its tracks . . . only three feet away.

Dad ran to shield Kevin. He aimed his rifle at the bear's head and pulled the trigger. But the gun jammed. He tried the lever again. But again it jammed. He poked the lifeless mass of fur with his barrel.

The bear was dead.

Dad turned and fell to his knees and threw his arms around his son. The trembling ten-year-old buried himself in his father's embrace. But after a few seconds, Kevin tore himself away.

"Wiggles!" he called out. Kevin limped to the

place the dog had fallen, while Dad steadied him. They dropped to their knees beside the limp, lifeless form.

Dad rested his hand over the dog's chest. "He's still breathing."

The dog didn't move. He didn't whimper. His eyes slit open just enough to reveal a flicker of life.

"Is he bad off, Dad?"

"I don't see any blood. But you can't always tell by that. Could be a ruptured organ, internal bleeding, broken back, any number of things."

They looked up to see the swinging light of a lantern coming toward them.

"Pete, you out there, Pete? Kevin?"

"Over here."

As the light came closer, it revealed the wispy form of Carl Matthews, lantern in one hand, rifle in the other.

"Thank God you're safe," he said, as if a great weight had been lifted from him. "Heard shots, and I rushed right over. Lucy said Kevin was lost, and somethin' about a bear."

"Right der Mizter Matt. He dead."

Mr. Matthews surveyed the animal. "Mighty mean lookin' bear. You okay, Kevin?"

"I otay. But Wiggles, he huwt. Huwt weally bad."

"How is he?"

86

"Hard to say, Carl. He's alive . . . barely. We best be gettin' 'em both home."

Dad carried Kevin on his back. Mr. Matthews carried Wiggles. They cushioned every step as they made their way over the pasture, careful not to jolt their precious cargo. Before long, they saw the diffused light of home. And like a lighthouse, it directed them safely through the thinning fog.

When Mom and Kim saw their forms emerge from the fog, they ran to meet them.

"Pete, is he—"

"He's all right, hun. A little shaken up, but he's all right."

"Thank God," Mom said.

"It's Wiggles dat's huwt, Mom. Huwt weally bad."

Dad and Mr. Matthews carried them inside. Dad laid Kevin on the couch. Mr. Matthews laid Wiggles next to him on the floor. Mom and Kim immediately attended to Kevin's ankle.

"Not me. I otay. Hep Wiggles."

Wiggles was unconscious. Gently, Dad moved his hands over the dog's body, feeling every bone, every joint, every vertebra.

"I don't think he has any broken bones."

He looked in his ears, his nose, his mouth.

"Doesn't seem to be any internal bleeding. At least, nothing I can tell."

"A good night's sleep might do him the best good," said Mr. Matthews.

"Good idea," Dad said.

"Can he stay in our room?" Kim asked.

"Not tonight. Let's put him in the laundry room," Mom said.

Dad dug his arms under the dog's legs and picked him up. Kim ran ahead and fluffed up the towels in the cardboard box. After Dad nestled him in the box, Mom turned off the light. Kim went over to the drawer, took out the nightlight, and plugged it in.

They looked at Wiggles for a moment, lying there, a huddle of helpless fur, so alone; their black bundle of boundless energy, now so limp and lifeless. They backed off, their hearts filled with fears of the worst. And they shut the door, leaving him to the mercy of the night.

Mr. Matthews gave the kids hugs before he left for home. He told Kevin not to worry and to get well soon. He squeezed Kim's hand, touched her cheek, and told her to be brave.

Dad went to fill the bathtub for Kevin. Mom reheated dinner, certain that once cleaned up, Kevin would be starved. But now he was resting on the couch. And he was starved for something more than food.

He reached out for Kim and hugged her. He

trembled in her arms, and her shoulder blotted his tears.

"It's all right, Kevin, everything's all right now. You're home."

He dried his eyes with the back of his hands.

"I awmost not come home, Kim. I awmost not ever see you again."

Then tears spilled over Kim's cheeks. "I don't know what I'd do if anything ever happened to you. I was so scared for you, out there in the fog, alone, and when I heard the shots, I, I—" He threw himself into her arms again.

They dried their eyes and looked at each other. Suddenly, they both burst out laughing. They laughed till they cried. And they cried until they had no more tears left to cry.

"Tell me about the bear."

"He was da biggest, meanest ting I ever did see. His head was *dis* big." He showed her with his hands. "And his claws were *dis* big. And his teeth gwowled and twied to eat me all gone."

"Really?"

"Weally. He chased me up a twee, and I couldn't go any taller up. He took a swing at me wit his paw. See?" He showed her the claw mark, crusted with dried blood. And the ankle.

Dad returned from the bathroom. "How about that bath now?"

Kevin smiled. "Otay, Dad."

He scooped Kevin up and carried him to the tub. He eased Kevin in, careful of his cuts and the gash on his ankle. With the warm water he washed the dirt from Kevin's wounds and, with some mysterious washcloth that only fathers have, he washed the fear from Kevin's heart.

"I ought to go up tomorrow and cut the head off that bear and get a taxidermist to mount it. It'd be a great trophy to hang in the den. Whaddya think?"

"No tanks, Dad. I don't tink I want him eye-bawlin' me all da time and gwowling his jaws at me evewytime I walk thwough da house."

"Don't blame you. Don't blame you a bit."

"I hope nobody ever gits dat mad at me again. I never seen anybody dat angwy before."

"God was good to you tonight, son."

"I know."

Mom popped her head into the doorway. "You boys hungry?"

"Starved," said Dad.

"Me, too."

The table was deliciously spread with a platter of steaming meatloaf, a mountain of mashed potatoes, a deep bowl of home-grown peas, sliced garden tomatoes, and hot buttered rolls. They took their seats around the table and bowed their heads as Dad prayed.

"Dear Father—"

He took a deep breath.

"Thank You . . . thank You for looking after our boy tonight—"

The rest of his words lodged in his throat, and he couldn't get them out. Kim peeked an eye open and looked at him, his eyes pressed closed, his head resting against folded hands. And he whispered, "Amen."

Back to School

That night everyone slept hard — except for Kevin. He thrashed around in his sleep and called out in the dark.

"Kevin," Kim whispered.

He kicked at his covers and called out again, "Go away. Go away!"

She got up to shake him awake, "Kevin. Kevin." His eyes rolled sleepily. His sheets were drenched with sweat. "It's okay, Kevin. It was just a nightmare. It wasn't real. Go back to sleep." She pulled the covers over his shoulders, kissed him on the forehead, and went back to bed.

Later that night Kim awoke and turned to check on Kevin. His bed was empty. She looked around. He was nowhere in sight. Suddenly wide awake, she pulled back her covers and walked anxiously down the hall to tell Mom and Dad.

But as she passed the laundry room, she noticed that the door was ajar. She looked inside. Kevin was lying on the floor next to Wiggles. Both were sound asleep.

Her first thought was to wake him up so he could crawl back into his warm bed. But a second thought came to her while she stood there.

She went back to her room and got Kevin's pillow and a blanket. She gently lifted his head and slid the pillow under it. Then she doubled the blanket and tucked it in around him.

The next morning the house awoke to the muffled sound of laughter from the laundry room. Wiggles had gotten up early and was licking Kevin's face all over to get him to wake up.

The night had been merciful. The sleep had done its work. Wiggles was fast on the road to recovery.

✳ ✳ ✳

September came too soon. It always does. But the nice thing was the twins' birthday. They were eleven now. And they were sixth graders. With sixth grade came a whole new set of things to adjust to—a different classroom, a different teacher, a whole new set of subjects with books to match.

94

A few things, though, remained the same. Same bus schedule. Same kids they had last year in class. And same old Jerrod. As luck would have it, he passed the fifth grade. They had to pass him. He was outgrowing his desk.

It was the first day of class and the twins mostly had to fill out forms and write their names in things and cover their books. But in the afternoon, the teacher asked the class to tell what they had done over the summer.

Billy had gone to Washington, D. C., and had toured the White House and the Smithsonian. Sarah had gone to Disney World. Jerrod had gone to summer school. *Reform school would have done him more good*, Kim thought.

When Kevin told about his summer, the other kids were soon on the edge of their seats. Everyone was captivated by his story. Even Jerrod sat up from his usual slouched position and listened.

While Kevin was talking, the kids around Kim kept turning to whisper things like, "Is that true? Did that really happen?" And she proudly nodded that, yes, it was all true and really did happen.

It was a small moment of glory for Kevin. After he finished, arms shot up all over class. Everyone was eager to ask him questions and pry out the details of his adventure.

From then on, it seemed, the class looked at

Kevin differently. He had fought off a bear. He had done something brave. The bravest thing any of them could boast about was not screaming on the roller coaster at Myrtle Beach.

✳ ✳ ✳

Autumn traveled through the valley like a gypsy artist, holding its palette of mixed paints in one hand and waving its wild brush with the other. A dab of crimson here. A broad stroke of burnt umber there. And before you knew it, the whole valley was a canvas full of fall colors.

It was November now. Green had given way to brown. Shirtsleeves had given way to sweaters. And Thanksgiving was just around the corner.

On the Saturday before Thanksgiving the Hallases were all working in the yard. Dad and Kevin were chopping firewood. Mom and Kim were raking leaves. Already they had dotted the yard with a dozen of the brittle piles.

Wiggles, meanwhile, had work of his own to do—chasing squirrels. The squirrels loved it. They dashed from tree to tree, scurrying up the trunk, just far enough up where Wiggles couldn't reach them. There they taunted him as he barked and jumped and frothed at the mouth in fits of frustration. They stared down at him with their calm brown eyes and mocked him with superior

96

twitches from their bushy tails.

It drove him crazy, but he thrived on the thrill of it all, and he endured all the humiliation on the hope of just once snapping his jaws down on one of their smart-aleck tails.

Amid this flurry of activity, Wiggles caught sight of some wild turkeys. They had crept warily to the barn to nibble from a sack of grain that had been torn open and spilled onto the ground.

Even more than chasing squirrels, Wiggles loved chasing chickens. And to him, turkeys were like chickens that had made it to the big leagues. He darted off toward the barn. The turkeys saw him and panicked.

Wiggles raced to cut off their escape route to the woods, and they tripped all over themselves trying to turn back. They gobbled so frantically you would have thought they had backed their tail feathers into a meat grinder.

He chased them toward the house. Must have been twenty of them. A few tried to break from the pack, but Wiggles cut them off and turned them back.

"Thanksgiving turkeys!" yelled Dad. "Grab one!"

The turkeys ran through the piles, kicking up leaves and adding to the confusion. When the family surrounded them, the turkeys bunched together into one big, hysterical huddle of feathers.

A few braver ones tried to make a run for it. Kevin dived at one, but missed.

"Got one!" Mom hollered. She'd caught it by the legs and immediately it started wildly flapping its wings. "Help, he's getting away!" The bird struggled to fly. Mom was on her tiptoes with her hands extended above her, fast losing her grip. By the time Kim got there to help, all she had was a fistful of feathers.

The turkeys took their cue and took to the air, making a frantic flight for freedom. Dad picked up the leaf rake and knocked one out of the air. Mom yanked a quilt from the clothesline and threw it over the disoriented turkey.

"Over here, kids, quick."

Kevin and Kim jumped on the quilt and held down the corners. Wiggles ran around, barking.

Feathers fell quietly to the ground as Dad drew in the quilt to contain the turkey. It kicked and flapped, but Dad finally subdued it. They all gawked at each other, amazed that they had actually caught one.

From a broken patch in the quilt, the turkey wormed his head out and looked as shocked to see them as they were to see him.

"Thursday, four o'clock. We'd love to have you over for dinner," Dad said to the turkey. It gobbled back defiantly and took a peck at Dad's nose.

Winter
in the Valley

November's leaves collected in tattered drifts throughout the valley. And there they stayed until December's winds swept them away. The ones not swept away got buried by snow.

One night while they slept, the snow came. Quietly. Elegantly. Like a white fur dropped on the valley from the shoulders of some heavenly snow queen. When they awoke the next morning, the twins couldn't wait to go out and play. To tramp through the snow and leave behind giant footprints. To build snowmen. To throw snowballs. To make snow ice cream. They just couldn't wait.

"Eat your breakfast first," said Mom. "Then you can go."

Breakfast was a steaming bowl of oatmeal

that had been cooked with raisins and tiny bits of apples. It swam deliciously in a moat of fresh cream and melted butter, topped with cinnamon and brownsugar.

When Kim and Kevin bundled up and went outside, the oatmeal felt like a warm stove in their stomachs. But after a couple of hours, the cold won out. They stomped the snow off their feet and came back inside.

Milking the gloves off their hands and shedding their coats, they crowded in front of the fireplace. There they pushed their throbbing hands against the crackling heat.

The hot chocolate Mom fixed helped. Kevin cupped his hands around the steaming mug and sipped just enough to bring his lips back to life.

"Kim, would you hep me wit my Chwistmas pwesents dis year?"

"What do you need?"

"For you to write da cards dat go wit da pwesents."

"Sure."

"Good. I see how much money I got in da pig."

They went to their room, where he poured out his piggy bank onto the bed. He counted the change, then dug inside for the dollar bills.

"Do you want me to help you pick them out, too?"

100

"Chur. All except yours."

"Let's make a list first." Kim got a pencil and sheet of paper from the desk. "Okay. Who all are you going to get presents for?"

"Wet's see. Mom. Dad. Mr. and Mrs. Matthews." He smiled. "And you, of course."

"Anyone else?"

"Wiggles. Can't fowget him."

"That's six presents. How much money do you have saved?"

"Exactwy twelve dollar and sixty-two cents."

"So that's about, mmm, somewhere around two dollars a present. That's your budget, okay?"

"Otay."

"Now, let's start with Mom. What do you want to get her?"

Kevin thought a while. "I don't know."

"How about Dad?"

"He's even hawder to buy for den Mom."

"How about Mr. and Mrs. Matthews?"

"Dunno. Maybe I get some ideas if I go to da stow and wook awound some. But I know what I want to get Wiggles."

That afternoon they persuaded Mom to drive them to the feedstore, where Kevin picked out a dog collar and got Wiggles' name engraved on it.

When they came home, Kevin went into the kitchen and opened the lower cabinet. It was filled

101

with empty oatmeal boxes.

"Mom been saving dem for me. I ask her to." He pulled one out and put the collar in it. "Now you do da note on da card, otay?"

He told Kim what to write, and she neatly printed it on the card. When she finished, she read it out loud and showed it to him. He was so proud of it. Then she dropped the card into the cylindrical box with the gift.

"Maybe wight befow Chwistmas I put in a couple bones, too. What you tink, Kim?"

"I think it's a good idea."

The next day, Dad and Kim went to chop down a Christmas tree while Mom and Kevin stayed inside to get the boxes of decorations down from the garage.

That night they trimmed the tree and strung the lights and set up the manger and hung their stockings by the fireplace. When they finished, Dad turned off the living room lights, and the family sat together on the couch to admire the twinkling tree with the star of Bethlehem beaming from its top branch.

In the morning Kevin went with Dad to buy Kim's present. Later that day he and Kim went with Mom to the grocery store for the others. They tumbled into the car and tagged along with her to see what the store had in the way of gifts.

"Can we wook awound da stow, Mom?"

"No, let's all stay together."

"But Mom—" he pleaded.

"I'll go with him. It'll be all right," Kim said.

"Well, okay. But don't take too long."

They hurried to the other side of the store. Kevin looked at a lot of girl things—makeup and perfume and things like that. His eyes were drawn to a compact mirror. He opened it up and saw himself. He smiled and moved the mirror all around his head. Then he used it to look over his shoulder. Then at the ceiling.

"Hurry, Kevin, she's standing in line."

They ran to the toy aisle where Kevin's eyes skittered over all the selections. Kim kept watch at the end of the aisle. He dawdled indecisively over the gifts but finally made his choices.

"Hurry, she's at the check-out stand."

Kevin brought the presents and ran to another check-out stand. The cashier totaled the merchandise. It came to $7.85. Kevin emptied his pockets and poured what he had onto the check-stand. The cashier patiently counted it.

"Seven-twenty-five . . . thirty-five . . . forty . . . fifty . . . fifty-one, two, three. Seven dollars and fifty-three cents." She looked up at Kevin. "You're thirty-two cents short."

Kim unsnapped her purse while Kevin fished

around in his pockets. He pulled them inside out, but he didn't find a cent. Fortunately, Kim found some change and gave it to the cashier.

"Here you go, thirty-two cents."

Kevin smiled at his sister. "I pay you back."

"That's okay."

As soon as they got home, they sneaked off to their room and poured out the sack onto the bed. For a few minutes they admired the purchases. Then they got down to business. Kevin told Kim exactly what he wanted written on the cards. She wrote while he scurried off to the kitchen to get the oatmeal boxes.

When they were finished stuffing everything into the boxes, Kim wrote names on the tops of every one: *Merry Christmas, Dad. From Kevin . . . . Merry Christmas, Mom. From Kevin . . .* and so on. Then they hid them away in the closet.

* * *

A few days before Christmas, Mrs. Matthews invited Kevin and Kim over to make cookies. They made them from scratch. Sugar-cookie Santas. Gingerbread reindeer. Oatmeal-cookie wreaths. And she let them decorate the cookies all by themselves.

Their last batch to decorate was the Christmas wreaths. After Kim painted them with green frosting, Kevin put the red hots on. He ate two for every one he put on, so they ended up running out of red hots before they ran out of wreaths.

When they finished, Mr. Matthews took Kevin into the den to show him a few tricks of the wood-carving trade. Kim stayed in the kitchen to help Mrs. Matthews clean up.

She poured two glasses of milk and put a few cookies on a plate. "'Thou shalt not muzzle the ox while he's threshing'—that's in the Bible. I think it means the cooks are entitled to first pick of the cookies." And with the childhood sacraments of cookies and milk, the years that separated them were bridged.

"He's a sweet boy, that brother of yours."

"I know."

"Does it ever bother you, him being the way he is?"

"It used to. Not so much anymore. But sometimes—" Kim paused to think. She hadn't ever shared this with anyone before. "—sometimes I wonder things."

"Like what?"

"Like why I got made normal and he didn't." Kim looked over at some of the burnt cookies they had decided not to frost. "Almost like these—cut out of the same dough, but left in the oven a little too long. Do you ever wonder about things like that, Mrs. Matthews?"

"I do. I wonder why we could never have children. Or why the one given to us was taken away."

"I wonder sometimes," said Kim, "why God didn't make Kevin normal, why He didn't take him out of the oven a little sooner."

"Well, maybe this is a better way to look at it, Kim. In one way, Kevin's a lot like this oatmeal box." She reached over and picked it out from the other boxes on the counter. "A little odd looking, isn't it?" Kim nodded. "Different from every other box I have. All the rest have squared corners and fit neatly on the shelf. This one doesn't fit in so well." She squeezed the box in with the others. "But it's not important that it's not like all the rest, not important that it doesn't fit like the others do. *How* it's packaged isn't nearly as important as *what* is packaged on the inside. And what's on the inside is good."

Kim listened intently. Then Mrs. Matthews passed her an oatmeal wreath.

"Here. Tell me what you think."

Kim took a bite of the cookie, chewed it, and savored its distinct taste. "Pretty good," she said with a smile.

"*Pretty* good?" She took a bite from Kim's cookie. "Why, it's delicious!"

And she was right, it was.

The Night
Before Christmas

I t was the night before Christmas and the stir-
ring of last minute preparations had not yet
stilled for the night. Packages were being wrapped,
tomorrow's food was being readied, and firewood
was being brought in to dry for an early morning fire.

Caught up in this blizzard of activity, Kevin
was busy with his own preparations. He rum-
maged through the drawers in his dresser, pulling
each one out and probing every inch. He found a
penny in the top drawer, a nickel in another, and
a penny in the bottom one.

Next he pulled at the handle of his desk
drawer, but it was so stuffed he could barely open
it. He yanked and yanked, and then it crashed to

107

the floor. Kevin shuffled through the mess and found a quarter. That was all he needed.

One by one he took the boxes down from the closet and wrapped them. When he came to Wiggles' box, he slipped into the kitchen and eased open the refrigerator door. He peered into its cool, cluttered shelves.

"What are you doing in there, Kevin?" asked Mom.

"Nuttin', Mom. Just gettin' weady for 'morrow."

He pulled something out and hid it behind his back as he hurried to his bedroom.

When Kevin and Kim finished wrapping the presents, they heard Wiggles in the living room, scratching on the door and whining to be let outside.

"What's wrong, boy?" asked Dad.

Wiggles ran around in circles, then scratched the door again and barked.

"I tink he got to go poddy. *Weally* bad."

Dad turned on the porch light, and they all looked out the window. There was a dog, sniffing around on the front porch. Wiggles jumped and pawed the door handle.

"Okay, boy, but don't stay out all night," said Dad.

He opened the door, and Wiggles bolted out. He skidded to a stop on the porch. Both dogs eyed

108

the other with hopeful caution and started sniffing each other.

Kevin cupped his hands against a window and saw the two running playfully through the snow.

"The call of the wild," Dad said with a smile as he reached his arms around Mom and gave her a kiss.

"Oh, Pete," Mom said, as she gave him a playful elbow in the ribs.

"Won't he git cold out der dis late at night in all dat snow?" Kevin was visibly worried.

"He'll be okay."

"But what if he gits lost like I did in da fog?"

"Look out there, Kevin. The moon is bright, and besides, animals are good about finding their way around in the dark. I don't think there's anything to be worried about."

Still, Kevin cupped his hands against the cold window, peering out to watch the dogs disappear into the moonlight.

"Bedtime, kids," announced Mom.

"It's only eight o'clock," Kim protested.

"I know, but we've got a full day tomorrow, and we'll all be up early."

"Just remember," said Dad, "the sooner you go to sleep, the sooner you'll get to wake up."

"Come on, Mom."

"No more arguing, Kim, it's bedtime."

109

Kevin still had his face pressed to the window. "Let's go, son, bedtime."

Dad tapped him on the shoulder. "He'll be all right, don't worry."

The twins shuffled off to bed, but it was a sleepless night for Kevin. He stared blankly at the ceiling. Thoughts of the time when he got lost in the fog came back to haunt him.

He remembered how disoriented he was. He remembered how scared he felt—and alone. He remembered the roar of the bear, piercing through the fog. He remembered the bear stalking him up the tree. Those angry eyes. Those terrible teeth. He remembered being on the ground, hiding behind the tree, and Wiggles plunging into the bear and knocking it down.

Suddenly he knew what he had to do.

Kevin crawled out of bed onto the cold, hard-wood floor, careful not to make it creak. He slipped into his clothes and tiptoed past the embers in the fireplace where the bulging stockings were all hung.

Ever so quietly he turned the knob on the front door and stepped out sideways through the narrow opening. The moon glistened on the snow. Kevin had no trouble following the tracks that trailed off into the distance.

But as he followed the trail, gusts of wind

kicked up flurries of the powdery snow and began to erode the tracks. Deeper into the valley he went. As he did, the night grew darker and the temperature, colder.

"Pwease, God, hep me find Wiggles. It getting so cold."

He looked down at the tracks, and they split in different directions. Kevin stood there confused.

"WIGGLES!" He paused for a reply. "WIGGLES!"

Still no reply. He followed the tracks that led deeper into the valley, instead of the ones that led up the foothills. Clouds clumped together in the sky to blot out the moon. The gathering darkness closed in around him. Kevin shuddered at the howl of a lone wolf in the distance.

The wind that had whistled around him grew more savage and biting. His cheeks burned. His fingers ached. His feet were numb.

"It stings so bad. Oh, Wiggles, where are you? Plwease come home," he said to the wind. But the wind nipped his fragile words right out of the air. He called out, "WIGGLES! WHERE ARE YOU? COME HOME, WIGGLES!"

Kevin burrowed his hands in his pockets and strained to find the trail. But the wind had whisked it away. He wandered aimlessly now and came to a ravine lined with jagged rocks and filled with thirty feet of darkness.

He stood on the lip of the ravine, squinting against the needles of snow that the wind threw at his face. He thought he saw something. He leaned over for a closer look. But when he did, he slipped and tumbled headlong into the dark chasm. He fell to the bottom of the ravine, unconscious.

Back on the front porch, Wiggles pawed at the door. Dad woke up and stumbled through the darkened house. When he unlatched the door, Wiggles ran inside, a shivering mass of wet, black fur. He trotted down the hall to the twins' room, and Kim heard him nosing around Kevin's bed. Then he barked.

"Shh, you'll wake Kevin," she said. He barked again. "Go to sleep, boy." But he barked again.

Dad came into the room to scold the dog, but when he did, he turned on the light and saw the empty bed.

"Where's Kevin?"

Kim sat up and rubbed her eyes. "He was here when I went to sleep."

Mom hurried into the room, cinching her robe.

"His coat's gone, and his shoes," Kim said. "They were right there when he went to sleep."

"Do you think he went looking for the dog?"

Their faces paled when they realized that he had. Dad ran and flung open the front door. A gust of wind sent it slapping against the wall. He saw the tracks. They were faint, but they were Kevin's.

"Get dressed, Lucy. I'll get the flashlight. Kim, you stay here and call the Matthews."

Dad and Mom headed out against the stiff wind with Wiggles by their side.

"Go find him, boy," shouted Dad, and he streaked through the snow on his trail.

The wind was really blowing now, sometimes stopping them in their tracks. They called out, but the wind and snow muffled their anguished attempts.

Within minutes, the Matthews came. Mrs. Matthews stayed inside with Kim while her husband joined the search. His lantern looked like a firefly weaving in and out over the snow as he ran to catch up.

By the time he reached Mom and Dad, they were at the top of the ravine. Wiggles had run to the bottom, and Dad was shining his light to find him. The dog barked. Dad jerked his light over to the left. There he saw Wiggles hunched over a motionless form.

"Oh, God," gasped Mom.

Dad hurried down the rocky slope, slipping as he went, until he reached Kevin. He checked his vital signs.

"He's alive, Lucy! He's alive!"

Mr. Matthews stood beside her, his lantern

illuminating the entire ravine. "I'm coming down."

"No, stay there, Carl. Too slippery. I can bring him up."

Dad held Kevin in his arms and carefully picked his way up the rocky incline to the top.

"How is he?" asked Mr. Matthews.

"Unconscious, but he's breathing."

Mom wrapped her scarf around his feet. Mr. Matthews threw his coat over Kevin's chest. Dad put his wool hat over Kevin's head.

"Let's get him out of this weather as quick as we can."

Long before they reached the house, Kim ran out to meet them. When they entered the house, they all helped strip Kevin down and placed him in bed. Mom called the doctor. Dad rubbed Kevin's hands and feet. The rest of them bustled around the house, filling hot-water bottles and finding heating pads.

It seemed like forever before the doctor arrived. When he did, it was all serious business. No smiles. No chitchat.

"How long was he out in the snow?" he asked.

"We think somewhere around an hour, hour and a half," said Dad.

"What was he wearing?" The doctor moved his stethoscope over Kevin's chest.

"Regular clothes," said Mom, "and a coat, but

no hat or gloves. And no socks. Shoes but no socks."

The doctor rolled back the covers to examine Kevin's feet. They were shades of bluish-gray and white. He turned to Kevin's head and probed it with his hands.

"We found him at the bottom of a ravine," Dad said. "He was out cold."

The doctor left the room and called for an ambulance. As he hung up, Dad asked, "How bad is he?"

"He has a bad concussion. Severe frostbite. Maybe some internal injuries, but we won't know that for sure till we get him to the hospital."

"What are his chances, doctor?"

"At best, he's probably going to lose his feet."

"And at worst?"

"With a concussion, it's hard to tell. Always the risk of a hemorrhage, swelling, coma. A lot of things can go wrong."

"Doctor!" yelled Mom from Kevin's bedside. "Come quick."

Everyone rushed into the bedroom to see Kevin's eyes fluttering. The doctor checked his pupils. Then Kevin regained consciousness.

He looked down by the bedside. "Wiggles," he said faintly. They all huddled around the bed and grabbed his hands. "Mom," he said with a weak smile.

"We're here, Kevin. Don't worry, we're all here."

He strained his eyes at the doctor.

"I'm Dr. Kellerman," he explained. "How are you feeling, son?"

"Not so good," he said. Kevin turned to Kim. "Can I have my wittle dog, Kim, da one Mizter Matt made me?" He pointed lamely over to the desk. She got it and handed it to him, and he clutched it tightly in his hand.

His eyes were heavy. Wiggles reached up and licked his hand. His eyes opened, and they all saw a little flicker of life return.

"Is it Chwistmas yet, Mom?"

"Almost, sweetheart, but not yet."

"Dad? Where's Dad?"

"Here. I'm right here." Dad squeezed his hand.

"Be sure evewyone gits der pwesents I got for dem."

"They'll be plenty of time for that later."

"Pwomise you do it?"

"Promise."

Kevin's eyes grew heavy and closed. His hand fell limp. The wooden dog dropped to the floor. Dr. Kellerman checked Kevin's eyes and hurried to put his stethescope on his heart. After a few seconds, he folded up his stethescope and backed away. He sighed heavily, then spoke.

"I'm sorry. We lost him . . . . He's dead."

Treasure
in an Oatmeal Box

Tears burst from Kim's eyes, and she cried out, "No. It's not true, it's not true." She threw herself over Kevin's chest and sobbed convulsively. "Come back, Kevin. Please. Please come back." She cried and she cried and she cried . . . onto a chest that didn't move.

Mom and Dad knelt down and put their arms around her. She turned to see their tears and collapsed into their arms.

The doctor and the Matthews huddled around them and shared their tears, clinging to the heartbroken family.

Finally the ambulance came. Dr. Kellerman took charge and handled all the details. The family regained their composure, but when Kim saw them carry Kevin out on the stretcher, covered with a sheet, she broke down. They all did.

The doctor left shortly after the ambulance. The Matthews left sometime later. And the family was left alone with their grief.

It was a long, hard night. The three of them sat in the living room, clumped together on the end of the couch. They sat in stunned silence, staring at the dying embers in the fireplace.

Wiggles came over to lick Kim's hand. He tilted his head to one side as if he didn't understand, as if to say, "What's going on? Where did Kevin go?"

"He's not coming back, boy." Kim's words crumbled as they left her lips. "He's not, he's not *ever* coming back." She hugged his neck and used it to blot her tears.

She crawled back on the couch, where she eventually fell asleep in her mother's arms. Dad carried her to bed. The hall light silhouetted him in the doorway as he stared at Kevin's empty bed.

He felt a painful emptiness, like an oyster suddenly pried open with a shucker's blade and mercilessly torn from its shell. But he was beginning to feel less the pain of the oyster and more the emptiness of the shell as he stared at the unmade bed.

He sat down on the oval rug that separated the twin beds and stared. That's all. He didn't think or pray or cry. He just stared.

118

Wiggles crawled up to him and placed his head on his lap. They were like two shells washed up on a deserted island—empty, still, and so alone.

Later that night Kim awoke and drowsily looked over at Kevin's bed. It wasn't empty. She could see his sleeping form lying there. *It had all been just a dream, just a terrible, terrible dream*, she thought to herself.

She went over to his bed to give him the biggest hug she had ever given him. "Oh, Kevin, I had the worst nightmare—"

When she said this, Wiggles lifted his head and looked at her with sad, dark eyes. It felt as if someone had suddenly dropped a red-hot coal into her heart.

She couldn't sleep there, not without Kevin in the room. She walked down the dark, creaky hallway—it seemed longer than it ever did before—and she crawled in bed with Mom and Dad.

The next morning a knock awakened them. Dad got the door. It was Mr. and Mrs. Matthews.

"Didn't mean to wake you up, Pete," said Mr. Matthews.

"That's all right."

"We brought some casseroles by and a little something for breakfast. Didn't think Lucy would feel much like cooking," said Mrs. Matthews.

"Thank you, Sadie, that was real sweet."

As they put the casserole dishes on the kitchen counter, Dad picked up Kevin's wooden dog.

"He would've wanted you to have this, Carl." Mr. Matthews extended his trembling hand. "It meant a whole lot to him." Tears pooled in Mr. Matthew's eyes. "*You* meant a whole lot to him." One of the tears trickled down the gulleys of his aging face. He bit his lip and nodded. And he put the little dog in his pocket.

"If there's anything we can do, call us," said Mrs. Matthews. "Okay?"

"We will," said Dad, and he walked them to the door.

When they left, Kim went into the kitchen and hugged Dad. Together they set the table. She reached into the cupboard and pulled out four plates. She put one at Dad's place, Mom's place, and her own.

She stood there with the extra plate, staring at it, and suddenly realized that they would not be setting a place for Kevin. Not for breakfast. Not for lunch. Not for dinner. Not ever.

The plate grew heavy in her hand. She turned from the table and returned it to the cupboard.

They all took their places around the table. Nobody talked. Instead of clinging to each other as they had the night before, it seemed as if they

121

all just wanted to be by themselves this morning, alone with their own thoughts.

They just picked at their breakfast. You could hear the scraping of forks against the plates, the crunch of toast, the sipping of coffee, but that was all.

Kim looked around the kitchen, mindlessly, numbly. The door was ajar to the cabinet that stored all of Kevin's oatmeal boxes. How he loved oatmeal. And how he loved to play with those silly looking boxes. He made drums out of them, stored crayons in them, used them to catch butterflies, even used some of them as bowling pins.

Kim excused herself from the table and went to her room. She looked around to see all that remained, all that Kevin left behind. A calendar picture of a black Lab pinned to his wall. A framed picture of a guardian angel guiding two children safely through a dangerous path. A family photograph. A shelf full of books, mostly stories about amimals and nature and fairy tales.

Strewn over the floor were Kevin's clothes. A litter of mismatched socks. A tangle of jeans. A wadded up T-shirt. Kim realized she would never have to pick up after him again. And her heart ached. She would clean up after him the rest of her life, just to have him back one more day, just to be able to tell him goodbye.

While she was taking inventory of her losses, Dad went for a walk.

He walked past the barn and paused as his eyes caught the twins' sled propped against the wall. It seemed so stiff, leaning against the red barn, drained of all its fun. It wasn't a sled anymore. It was just wood and metal and a little piece of rope, that's all.

He walked a ways past the barn and came to Kevin's special place near the oak tree. The leafless oak stood like a skeleton. His eyes followed the thinning branches into the sky. There was no blue in the sky and no yellow from the sun. There was only gray—an impenetrable gray spread over all the heavens.

Back home, Mom went on a walk of her own throughout the house, going from room to room, picking up memories of Kevin like so many clothes from the floor.

She looked down at the rug in front of the fireplace that had hosted so many wrestling matches and storytimes and late-night snacks.

She walked to the kitchen and looked at the table. At one time, she thought she would go crazy if she had to wipe up one more puddle of Kevin's spilled milk. Now, she would have given anything to have him spill it just one more time.

Mom pulled out a chair and sat down. Her eyes

looked over the room. Those dirty fingerprints on the refrigerator were Kevin's. You wouldn't think dirty fingerprints would be precious to a mother. But these were. They would be so painful to wash off this time.

She got up and walked down the hall. She stopped at the laundry room. She opened the swinging door and looked in. Her eyes trudged through the room, picking up more memories. Wiggles' bowl. The night light. The old clock. These fragments of a happy past lay all around her, like shattered pieces of a vase.

Finally, she came to Kim's room.

"You okay?" she asked.

"No."

"Want to talk?"

"No," Kim answered, then changed her mind, "Yes. Where was God last night, Mom? Why didn't He protect Kevin like He did from the bear?"

"He must have felt it was time for Kevin to come home, like when Daddy calls you in from play to come home for supper."

"But this is home, here, isn't it?"

"This is just a temporary home, where we stay for a little while till we finally arrive at our *real* home in Heaven."

"Will we know Kevin when we get to Heaven?" she asked.

"Oh, yes. We'll know him and talk with him and laugh with him and hug him. But it may take us a little while to recognize him, because he'll be different."

"Different? You mean like not being handicapped?" asked Kim.

"Yes, I'm sure of it. He'll be whole and well and strong," said Mom.

"I'm happy for him then. I would like to see him run up there, in Heaven. He always had trouble with that here. But, Mom, I'm still gonna miss him so much. I'll even miss the way he used to run. And how he talked. And how we used to tickle each other's arms at night."

"We'll all miss him, hun. There'll be an empty bed in all of our hearts," said Mom as she looked over to Kevin's bed.

Kim buried her face in Mom's chest and cried, "Oh, Mommy, Mommy, it hurts so bad."

"I know. I know it does, sweetheart." And they cried together in each other's arms.

"It may be good where Kevin is now," said Kim as she dried her tears, "but it'll never be good here without him. It hurts too much to be good."

"I know it's hard to understand right now, but God can make it good. He promised that all things work together for good for those who love Him. That doesn't mean that all things that happen to us *are* good, but they work *for* good, if we let them.

"I don't understand," Kim said.

"It's something like baking a cake from scratch. All kinds of things go into it. Flour. Baking powder. Eggs. Milk. Butter. Sugar. When all those things get stirred up and put in the oven, then you have cake."

"I still don't understand."

"Not all of the ingredients that go into a cake taste good. Some we would never choose to eat by themselves. Who would want to eat a mouthful of flour or a raw egg? If we had our choice, we'd probably just pick the milk and sugar, the sweet things. But that would never make a cake, would it?"

Kim shook her head no.

"Kevin's death is like a mouthful of flour—it's hard for us all to swallow. But God can use even Kevin's death, as it's mixed into our lives, to bring about something good."

"I guess I'm having a hard time mixing the flour. Mine must have a lot of lumps."

"That's all right, Kim. It'll mix in time. You can't rush what the Lord's doing in a person's life anymore than you can rush a cake made from scratch. Some things just take time."

Dad stomped his feet off on the front porch and came in the house to put a few logs in the fireplace.

Mom and Kim came in the living room to sit beside him on the couch.

"Kim has some questions I thought you could help her with, Pete."

"Sure, hun," he said to Kim, "go ahead."

"Why is it that God didn't answer our prayers about Kevin? He listened when we prayed for Kevin when he was lost in the fog last summer, but this time, He didn't."

"Do you think I would ever not listen if you came crying to me for help?"

Kim shook her head no.

"Do you think God is less of a father than I am?"

Again, she shook her head.

"Then He would never ignore us if we needed His help, would He?"

"No," Kim said, "I guess not."

"It's because He *is* a father and is in the process of raising us that He must answer in ways that are hard for us to understand. If you asked me for candy at the store, and I knew Mom had dinner waiting on the table when we got home, I would say no. Not because I didn't want you to enjoy the candy, but because I understand what is waiting for you down the road. And what's waiting for you down the road is food far better for you than candy. Food that your body needs to grow.

127

So when God says no, it's not because He doesn't care or isn't listening."

"Yeah, but, Dad, we asked Him for something more important than candy. We asked Him for Kevin."

"Maybe that should tell us something about why He said no. Maybe God has a bigger purpose for Kevin than to just be your brother or my son. Maybe God could do more through Kevin's death than through his life. Maybe it's His way of sparing Kevin some future pain, I don't know."

"Those are a lot of maybes, Dad. Which is it?" asked Kim.

"I don't know. Maybe *not* knowing is part of His purpose for us. Maybe we won't know till we look back years from now. And maybe we'll never know until we get to Heaven. Like looking in a two-way mirror. We may never see anything but ourselves until we go to the other side and look back."

Just then the phone rang, and Mom called to Dad. It was the funeral home. The service would be day after tomorrow.

The next day was spent with visitors and phone calls and people dropping off food. The pastor came by, too. All the company seemed to lessen the pain, but then one of them would start to cry, and it was like taking the bandage off a fresh cut. It started bleeding all over again, and the pain came back, all tender and exposed.

But the tears grew fewer and farther between. It was like they were all bottled up in this well of pain somewhere deep inside you, and when the tears came out, the well got smaller.

Snow was still on the ground the day of the funeral, but the sun was out, and it wasn't cold. People came from all over the valley. Even Jerrod Jackson came, dressed in a suit. He came by afterwards and told Kim how sorry he was. And she could tell he really meant it, because he had to fight back his tears to tell her.

Later in the day when the last of the people were leaving, Dad asked the Matthews to stay.

"I promised Kevin I would make sure his gifts were all distributed. If you all could stay a little while longer, I'd be grateful."

Carl and Sadie took their seats on the couch.

"Besides our family and Wiggles, you two were probably the closest friends Kevin had. As his father, I want to thank you. Means a lot to me, to all of us."

"He was an easy person to love," said Mrs. Matthews.

Mom and Kim gathered the oatmeal boxes from the closet and brought them into the living room. They placed them next to Dad, on the hearth.

"For you, Sadie," Dad said as he handed her the box.

She slowly slipped the ribbon off and opened the top. She pulled out a delicate hanky, embroidered with little roses in one corner. Then she took out the note printed on the small card. It read:

Sadie is a very pretty name and you are a very pretty person. I hope you like this. You can use it to blow your nose or to wipe sweat away or for tears and things like that.
Your friend,
Kevin

Never did she need a gift like this as much as she needed it now.

Dad gave the next box to her husband. He opened it and pulled out a nest made of real twigs with two little birds sitting in it. The note read:

This made me think of you two lovebirds. They don't have any babies in their nest either. But they love each other. That's what's really important.
Your friend,
Kevin

Reluctantly, Mom opened hers next. She took out a mirror, then the notecard:

130

Look at this and you will see the sweetest
woman in the whole world. I hope I marry
someone sweet as you someday.
Your son,
Kevin

She looked in the mirror and saw tears stream-
ing down her face, tears for the wedding that would
never be, for the "someday" that would never come.

Dad opened his next. He looked at a plastic
bear and read the note:

Remember this old bear? We showed him,
didn't we, Dad? When I grow up, we can hunt
bears again sometime. Okay?
Your son,
Kevin

He squeezed the bear so tightly his hand began
to shake. A tear took a quiet path down his face for
the "sometime" he knew would never come.

He gave Kim her box and the one for Wiggles.
She emptied Wiggles' box and out tumbled two
meaty rib bones, along with a beautiful dog collar
with a shiny, engraved tag. She put it around his
neck. It read simply:

To Wiggles from Kevin,
I love you.

131

Wiggles paraded his new collar around the room for all to see.

Now it was Kim's turn. She opened the box and turned it upside down. Out rolled thirty-two cents, followed by a white diary with a gold key. The note was in Dad's handwriting:

> To help you remember the important things you never want to forget.
> Your brother,
> Kevin

The diary would always have a special place in Kim's heart. She would never forget her twin brother or the important things that his gentle life had taught her.

The room was silent, each person cherishing their own treasure in the oatmeal box that Kevin had given them. But in the unspoken regions of their heart, they knew that the treasure in the oatmeal box was not the *gift* they had received that Christmas.

It was the giver.

Kevin was the real treasure. And they knew that as long as they had memories of him, their lives would always be rich.